S0-AGY-230

Oh My!
It Must Be The Sky!
Written By
Laura Appleton-Smith
Illustrated By
Preston Neel

Laura Appleton-Smith was born and raised in Vermont and holds a degree in English from Middlebury College. Laura is a primary schoolteacher who has combined her talents in creative writing and her experience in early childhood education to create *Books to Remember*. Laura lives in New Hampshire with her husband Terry.

Preston Neel was born in Macon, GA. Greatly inspired by Dr. Seuss, he decided to become an artist at the age of four. Preston's advanced art studies took place at the Academy of Art College San Francisco. Now Preston pursues his career in art with the hope of being an inspiration himself; particularly to children who want to explore their endless bounds.

A Book to Remember™
Published by Flyleaf Publishing
Post Office Box 287, Lyme, NH 03768

For orders or information, contact us at **(800) 449-7006**.
Please visit our website at **www.flyleafpublishing.com**

First Edition
Library of Congress Catalog Card Number: 2003096688
Hard cover ISBN: 1-929262-20-5
Soft cover ISBN: 1-929262-21-3

For Laura K., my right hand woman, my friend, and my talented designer.
Thank you for all that you do. This one is for you!

LAS

For the dragon in all of us.

PN

Once upon a time Lucky Ducky was swimming
in the pond when PLUNK, a nut dropped
and hit him smack-dab on the top of his crest.

“Golly!” Lucky Duck quacked.

He did not know what had hit him,
but he did know that he felt a bit dizzy and groggy.

Henny Penny spotted Lucky Ducky as he swam around and around in the pond.

"Luck, Luck, Lucky Duck," Henny Penny clucked,
"Why do you swim willy-nilly, willy-nilly?
Why are you acting so silly, silly, silly?"

"I got hit on the crest, but I do not know by what," quacked Lucky Duck.

"Oh my, it must be the sky!" Henny Penny clucked with a cry, "We must tell the King!
The sky is falling! The sky is falling!"

"Quick, quick, quickly Lucky Duck, put on this helmet,"
Henny Penny clucked as she put half of a nut
on top of Lucky Duck's crest.

She put the other half on herself;
then they ran and flapped off to tell the King.

Just then they met Fretty Froggy on the bank of the pond.

“Hop Fretty Froggy, hop. This is bad, bad, bad…
Lucky Ducky was out for a swim
when the sky fell smack-dab on his noggin.
We must tell the King that the sky is falling!”

Fretty Froggy began to cry.

"Try, try, try not to cry," clucked Henny Penny,
"Put on this helmet and hop with us–
get, get, get to the King fast we must!"

So off they ran and flapped and hopped until they bumped into Funny Bunny and Silly Filly.

When Funny Bunny and Silly Filly spotted Henny Penny and Lucky Ducky and Fretty Froggy with their helmets on they cracked up.

They snickered and giggled until they fell
on the grass and wiggled.

“This is not a funny, funny matter,” clucked Henny Penny,
“Lucky Ducky got hit in the noggin with a bit of sky
and Fretty Froggy began to cry. We must tell the King
that the sky is falling. The sky is falling!”

Well, Silly Filly and Funny Bunny
did not know if they should giggle or run,
but they felt that the trip to visit the King
would be fun…

So they put on a bucket and a cup as helmets
and they went off to tell the King.

Next the gang ran into the Sly Fox,
who sat next to a bubbling crock.

“Quick, quick, foxy fox,” Henny Penny clucked,
“Do not dilly dally. You must rally, rally, rally.
We must tell the King the sky is falling!”

You must understand that Sly Fox was a bit giddy
at his luck.

He inspected the gang and licked his lips
thinking of his suppers of rabbit, hen, frog's legs and duck.

But as Sly Fox sat thinking of his tummy,
Silly Filly snuck up in back of him
with a plan that was funny...

"Foxy must put on a helmet," she giggled as she dumped the liquid from the crock and dropped the pot onto the fox.

Sly Fox did not understand what had hit him.
"It must be the sky," Sly Fox said with a cry.

"Yes!" the gang yelled in reply,
"We must tell the King the sky is falling!
The sky is falling!"

So off tromped the gang up into the craggy hills
where it was windy and frosty.

They dropped down
into the foggy bog
where it was soggy
and sloppy.

“I am stuck,”
quacked Lucky Duck,
who had sunken down
into the messy muck.

Just then, the kingdom's BIG UGLY DRAGON turned up...

The dragon sniffed at Lucky
and professed him to be "Yummy,"
then he licked his lips and rubbed his tummy.

The gang gasped as the dragon puffed
a gust of hot wind from his nostrils.

"Pick, pick, pick on a duck your own size,"
clucked Henny Penny as she tapped her wing
on the dragon's back.

This stopped the dragon in his tracks.

Had he ever met a duck as big as himself?

"You are a big, big bully. It is a bad habit
to pick on an itty bitty duck.
We must not dilly dally. Get, get, get to the King
fast we must," Henny clucked.

“I am sorry,” said the dragon.

He puffed a soft puff of wind at the messy muck.
The mud turned to dust, and out stepped Lucky Duck.

"Thanks Dragon," quacked the little duck,
"You were a big help getting me out of that muck.
Do you want to be my buddy?"

It was as if the sun had melted the big ugly dragon...
He was so happy, he lifted his little buddy in his hand
and summoned the rest of the gang.

"Hop on,"
he said
as he lifted
his wings,
"I will fly you
to the King."

With his spyglass, the King spotted the dragon flying in.
He was fed up.

You see, the dragon had a bad habit of huffing
and puffing around and terrifying the kingdom.

Once and for all, the dragon must be stopped.

The King summoned fifty of his best men.
He jumped on his trusty donkey, and galloped off
to confront the dragon at the kingdom's entry.

The King and his men
were flabbergasted
to see the dragon
standing with
a granny hen,
a fluffy bunny,
a pretty filly,
a slippery frog,
a giddy fox,
and an itty bitty duck.

This was when Henny
Penny stepped up…

"Oh Lofty King of Dignity," Henny Penny clucked as she tipped her helmet from her crest, "My humble gang has traveled up hills and into soggy bogs to tell you that the sky is falling."

"And the DRAGON?" asked the King.

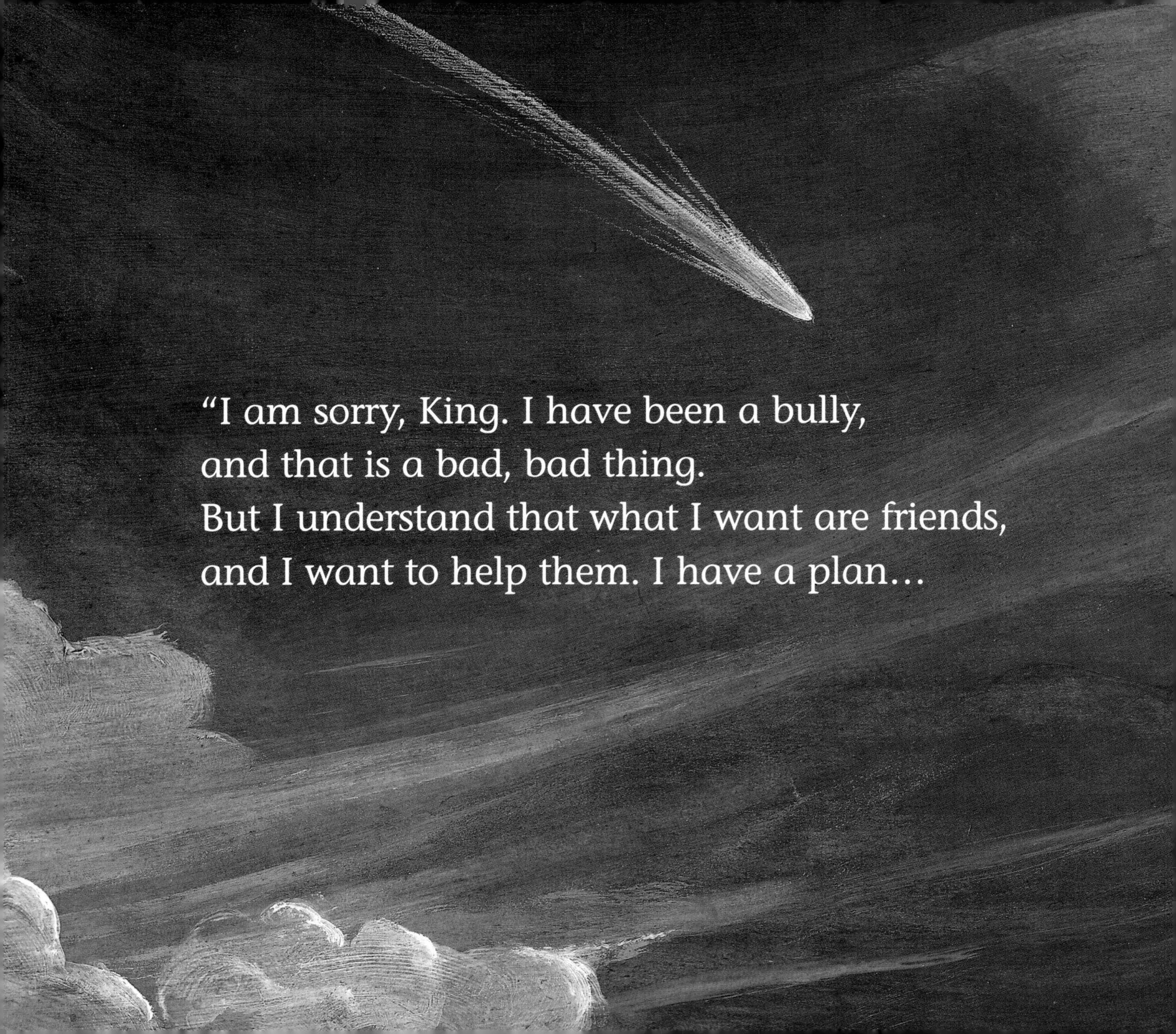

"I am sorry, King. I have been a bully,
and that is a bad, bad thing.
But I understand that what I want are friends,
and I want to help them. I have a plan...

Day and night I will fly to protect the kingdom
and my friends from the falling sky."

The King was so happy with his luck.
The ugly dragon's bullying had stopped
and he would protect the kingdom if the sky dropped.

The King let out a cry, "This calls for a festival!"

"Hip-hip for our buddy the dragon!"
The gang and the King's men yelled in reply.

The dragon was so happy he began to cry.

It was a grand festival.

Henny Penny, Lucky Duck, and the rest of the gang got silver helmets to protect them if the sky should fall...

And they lived happily ever after, one and all.